The Road to After

The Road to After

written and illustrated by

REBEKAH LOWELL

NANCY PAULSEN BOOKS

NANCY PAULSEN BOOKS

An imprint of Penguin Random House LLC, New York

First published in the United States of America by Nancy Paulsen Books,
an imprint of Penguin Random House LLC, 2022

Text and illustrations copyright © 2022 by Rebekah Lowell

Visit us online at penguinrandomhouse.com

Library of Congress Cataloging-in-Publication Data
Names: Lowell, Rebekah, author.
Title: The road to after / Rebekah Lowell.
Description: New York: Nancy Paulsen Books, [2022] | Summary: Eleven-year-old Lacey
rediscovers life and the soothing power of nature and art after she, her little sister, and
her mom escape from their controlling and abusive father.
Identifiers: LCCN 2021032523 | ISBN 9780593109618 (hardcover) |
ISBN 9780593109625 (ebook)
Subjects: CYAC: Novels in verse. | Survival—Fiction. | Psychological abuse—Fiction. |
Psychotherapy—Fiction. | Family life—Fiction. | LCGFT: Novels in verse.
Classification: LCC PZ7.5.L68 Ro 2022 | DDC [Fic]—dc23
LC record available at https://lccn.loc.gov/2021032523

Book manufactured in Canada

ISBN 9780593109618

1 3 5 7 9 10 8 6 4 2

FRI

Design by Marikka Tamura
Text set in Plantin MT Pro

For my daughters, Elektrah and Ariah—
you gave me the strength to take the first step.
And for the community who came together to help set us free.
We are forever grateful.

*T*hose who contemplate the beauty of the earth find reserves
of strength that will endure as long as life lasts. . . . There
is something infinitely healing in the repeated refrains of
nature—the assurance that dawn comes after night, and
spring after the winter.

—Rachel Carson

PART ONE

Sprouting

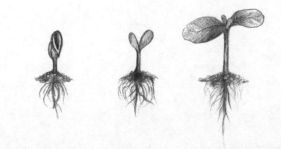

The FIRST STEP

Thunder
banging on the door.
Voices yelling—
like lightning.
But—
Daddy already left for work.
A loud crack tells me
the door to outside is wide open.
Light pours in.

VISITORS

Who is here? I dash to the edge of the stairs to see.

"Lacey," says Mama, running up. "Get ready. We have
to go now."

I freeze.

"Your grandparents are here to help us leave."

Leave?

We're not supposed to go anywhere.

We're not supposed to leave!

We never leave home without Daddy.

"Now!" Mama tosses a bag to me.

"Put on your shoes!"

My little sister screams, curling her toes.

Jenna won't let Mama put on her shoes.

She knows the rules too.

Shoes mean going out—

and we cannot go out without Daddy.

"You didn't tell me we were leaving!" I scream.

Mama replies, "I couldn't—

it wasn't safe then."

INVASION

Tall men in black boots come up the stairs.
Footsteps like a storm.
THUD!
CRASH!
CRACK!
Their metal badges shine even in our dim room,
where dark-brown fabric is pinned over the windows
to keep out the light, the way Daddy wants it.
I stare—at them, at their guns.
Daddy wears his on a sling, or leaves it in the fruit bowl,
and he yells at us if we touch it.
"You have five minutes," one of them warns.
As quick as I can, I cram things into the bag,
but it's not easy with shaking hands.
Suddenly, my grandmother comes upstairs,
rushing past the men to give Mama a hug.
But Mémère isn't supposed to be here!
Daddy says she's not allowed.
If Daddy comes back now—
The thought fills me with fear.
My face feels cold; my feet won't move.
I'm planted here, like a tree.
Mama reaches for my hand.
"It's okay," she says, looking into my eyes.
"We're going to be okay."

RULES

Daddy has many rules,
but Mama has rules too.
We just have to do exactly what Daddy says—
stay quiet, stay inside,
and if he wants to play,
play along.
If we follow these rules,
everything will be fine.
Leaving breaks Mama's most important rule
about how to stay safe.
Mama changed the rules and didn't tell me.

SAVING SOME THINGS

"Stick them onto what you want to bring," Mémère says,
handing us each a small stack of bright-pink paper squares.
I mark the framed pictures of our baby feet,
Jenna's blanket and blocks, my little deer I named Diamond,
my drawings, Mama's paintings, boxes stacked in a corner.
Then I remember my nature journal.
I find it tucked under my mattress,
where I hid it from Daddy.
Instead of tagging it, I place it in my bag.
But where's Mac?
I look around the room for our dog.
"Mac!" I call out over and over again.

NOW!

"There's no time for that! We have to
get you out before he comes back,"
the tall men roar as loud as Daddy.
I cover my ears with my hands.
Other men rush by, taking out boxes and boxes.
Daddy's long guns. Daddy's short guns.
They are even dropping boxes out the windows
that Daddy always kept closed.
Where are they taking everything?
And us?
"Let's go!"
"NOW!"
Their voices boom over Jenna's crying.
Even though my head is spinning,
somehow I make it downstairs without falling.
Pépère meets me at the bottom.
"Okay, let's go, kiddo," he says.
Muddy boots have stomped
all over the thunderstorm drawings
that I was making with Jenna
on the kitchen floor this morning.
Our drawings, stomped over.

LEAVING

"Mac!"

Our dog appears out of nowhere.

He runs to me, shaking, tail tucked in,

and I stick a pink paper square on him.

Daddy says Mac is his, but Daddy is mean to him.

Mac whimpers while I rub his soft head.

"Don't worry, bud. You're coming with me."

We walk toward the open door together.

The bright sunlight hurts my eyes,

making it hard to see.

I hold on to Mac with one hand

and Mama with the other

as we step outside, down the broken steps

that Daddy never fixed.

Our feet slop across the mud in our yard.

That means it's springtime in Maine.

The driveway is full of muddy tire tracks.

Daddy will notice that.

He's going to be so mad that people were here

while he was gone.

In the DRIVEWAY

Pépère opens his car door for me.

White teddy bears are on the seats.

"What about Jenna's car seat?" I ask.

"She has a new car seat," he says.

"Daddy's going to be so mad," I say.

"It's okay," Mama says as she buckles Jenna in.

"Don't worry about what Daddy will think."

But what Daddy thinks

is what we *always* worry about.

I take a step into the car and turn to help Mac up,

but a man outside the car puts his hand through Mac's collar,

holding him back.

"He can't go with you now," he says, pulling Mac away.

"We have to get you to safety first."

"No!" I scream as he shuts the car door.

"Mac!"

My heart twists.

"Mama!" I plead, looking at her.

Her eyes fill, but she says nothing,

wrapping her arm around me.

I stare through the window at Mac.

He's trying to wiggle away.

We drive off with white teddy bears on our laps

onto a road we've never been on without Daddy.

HEARTS

My sister's bear holds a red heart in its paws.

My bear's heart is hot pink.

Both hearts have the word LOVE

written on them and have soft lace trim.

LOVE.

Daddy doesn't allow us to use that word.

He won't give us permission to love.

But I secretly love Mac, even without permission.

I love Diamond too.

Daddy doesn't think we should have dolls

or stuffed animals, like Diamond.

When I was five, he threatened to throw Diamond away.

"If you want to keep Diamond safe,"

Mama warned, "keep her hidden when Daddy's home.

Never let him see how much you love her."

By following Mama's rules, I kept Diamond safe

and I kept my nature journal safe.

But how am I supposed to keep Mac safe?

Is Mama breaking a rule to keep us safe?

The POLICE STATION

Mémère and Pépère wait in the car.
Jenna is in Mama's arms as we follow a man into a
brick building,
up some stairs, and into a room with too-bright lights.
They close the door and it slams, making me flinch.
Mama tries to put Jenna down, but she cries,
so Mama has to pick her up again.

There's a big whiteboard and some markers
in the back of the room, and the man says we can draw.
That reminds me of the drawings I made
in my secret place in the bathroom closet.
There, I could close the door and draw—
birds, flowers, ladybugs, and the sun.
Now I wonder if I'll ever see them again.

I bring Jenna to the whiteboard with me.
She scribbles at the bottom where she can reach,
then shows me a heart she's drawn
like the ones on our new teddy bears.
I make myself smile for her.
Jenna doesn't talk.
She's four years old and never has.
I don't know if it's because she doesn't know how
or doesn't want to.

I wonder sometimes, if she did talk,
what would she say?
Maybe it's easier to keep
all the hurt in?

I LISTEN *to* THEM TALKING

The man sitting with Mama at the table says he's
Trooper Podos.
He takes out a small machine and sets it on the table.
Says he needs to ask Mama few questions, and
is it okay if he records?
Mama nods.
"How long have you been unable to leave?" he asks.
"Thirteen years," Mama says softly.
"Can you tell us about what occurred to make you decide
to leave now, after all this time?" he asks.
"He said he had to fix their teeth," Mama says, then adds,
"He bought a dental hand piece, a drill.
And he intended to use it."
Trooper Podos looks stunned.
"I had to protect them. Things were getting worse."
Mama looks like she's going to cry when she adds,
"I couldn't let him . . ."
I look back and forth at them from where
I stand at the whiteboard with Jenna.
"Things will be better now," Trooper Podos says,
and I wonder what things will be better now
if everything I know is gone?
Trooper Podos leaves the room, but quickly comes back to say
they just found Daddy and took him to jail.

OFF BALANCE

Things *were* beginning to get worse.
I remember something sharp and painful.
WHACK!
Daddy hit me, and I was too stunned to move.
Could only watch him lift his arm again,
high in the air, ready to strike another time.
Mama ran to stand between us.
"Stop!" she pleaded. "That's enough!"
"Oh yeah? Says who?"
He got closer to her face, loomed bigger.
Jenna cried for Mama from the floor.
Daddy picked her up, and she screamed more.
Mama reached for Jenna, helpless.
Daddy snarled, "Don't think of challenging me."
But then he passed Jenna into Mama's open arms.
"Why would I want this whiny baby, anyway?"
Daddy walked away back to his chair, turned on the TV.
I remember letting out the breath I didn't know I was holding.
And after all this time, I still don't know what I did
to make him mad that time.

HURT

Now my daddy's in jail.
I just want to know
why we couldn't have
just talked to him
to get him to change.

For ME

We leave the police station and return to
Mémère and Pépère's house.
When we arrive, Pépère hands me an envelope.
My name is written on it in beautiful letters.
"We know your birthday was last week," Mémère says,
"and that you couldn't have cards before,
but we thought maybe now it's okay."
I open it, and inside there's a card with a picture
of cake with candles on it.
"Thank you," I say.
I've never had a cake with candles on it before.
I've never even had a birthday card before,
because we weren't allowed to have birthdays.
Another rule broken.

CONFUSION

I used to know what to do to stay on Daddy's good side.
Every night when we heard his truck coming
up the driveway, we stopped everything.
I hid my book, put away Jenna's blocks,
our crayons, our pictures.
I brushed my hair, and Jenna's.
Mama changed and put on her earrings.
We knew what to do.
We knew how to do things right.
And if we messed up,
we knew how to fix it.
Now all I know is we live on the other side
of the rules I thought I knew.

TOO MUCH

The doorbell rings again and again.

"Friends," Mémère says.

They bring us food and toys and too much noise.

I cover my ears but can't help hearing them talking.

At least *before* the daytime was quiet

when Daddy was at work.

And we knew that if we just did the right things,

he wouldn't be too mad when he got home at night.

Why couldn't we go back and keep doing that?

"What a shame," one woman says. "Poor kids!"

"He seemed like such a nice young man," says another.

"He was such a charmer."

"A hard worker."

"But keeping Charlotte and the girls shut up like that."

"At least they're safe from him for now."

"It's good he's in jail."

I run upstairs to find Mama.

She hasn't come out of our bedroom for days.

She's not talking. Not eating. Not caring.

I open the door and she's sitting on the bed,

staring at the wall.

Jenna's on the floor,

and even though our room's full of new toys,

she's playing with our old blocks—

the ones Daddy almost put into the fire.

All of a sudden I need to scream.

"You made Daddy go to jail," I yell at Mama.

"You made us lose Mac."

My heart pounds.

She looks up at me, blank faced,

and with her silence, I explode.

"You did this," I holler. "It's all your fault!"

Then I hit Mama.

My hand stings.

I hold my breath.

Jenna looks up at me

as her block tower tumbles over.

BAKING

Mémère is baking, and the whole house
smells like a cinnamon-vanilla hug.
This is something new—
back home, we didn't have a mixer
or ingredients to bake.
I nod when my grandmother asks if I want to help.
"This was your mama's when she was little," she says
as she places an apron over my head
and ties it in the back.
We measure and pour, mix and blend,
and then, in twelve minutes, we have the first
chocolate chip cookies I've ever tasted.
They are my new favorite food.
Mama finally comes downstairs.
Maybe it was the smell of our cookies?

BITTERSWEET

Mémère asks us if we want to go for a drive.

Mama doesn't say anything, but I see her put on her coat,

getting ready to leave, so I find my coat too.

Going out reminds me of how Daddy used to change when

we were in public—how he acted all nice.

He smiled at cashiers and joked with us,

so we smiled too, pretending we were a happy family.

I always tried to make being around other people last longer,

because as soon as we'd get back into the truck,

the mean daddy would return.

"Did you see how helpful that cashier was, Lacey?

She's not lazy and useless like your mother.

You want to grow up to be like her—not your mama."

I just nodded. I knew better than to say anything back.

Because the one time I defended Mama,

he didn't talk to me or look at me for days.

Now that we've left, I'm sure about only one thing—

Daddy will never look at me

or talk to me

or love me ever again.

Even if I never knew whether he loved me for sure,

I liked to think he did.

I wish I'd been able to say goodbye.

IN-BETWEEN

We go to Fortunes Rocks Beach and walk
on the wet packed sand at low tide
in the cold breeze.
The line between ocean and sky grays out.
I skip a stone and it bounces away into forever.
The beach is empty, just like I feel—
gray and cold.
Gray is an in-between color.
That's what I am—
in-between.

WILD

I watch out my window on the drive home.
Rows of power lines connect one to another.
Daddy used to take us blueberry picking.
Daddy, Mama, Jenna, and me,
all hiking together along the power line path.
Like a family.
Daddy and Mama each had a bucket.
Plink, plank, plunk,
the berries dropped in, small and indigo blue.
Jenna and I didn't need a bucket.
We ate everything we picked.
Orange-red tiger lilies spotted the pathway, and
Daddy stopped, picked one, and held it out to me.
"For you."
A small space in the middle of my chest ached
knowing this side of him would fade
sooner than the flower.

NIGHT SOUNDS

At night, Mama holds us in her arms as we fall asleep,

and the soft sounds of Pépère and Mémère talking

downstairs help me drift off to sleep.

But tonight I wake and hear Mama's voice downstairs too.

I get up, tiptoe down the hallway,

and sit at the top of the stairs to listen.

"Thank you, Officer," I hear Mama say. "What about Mac?"

"His brother came to get him," a deep voice responds.

Mama mumbles words I can't hear.

"Don't say that, ma'am," the policeman says.

"Your husband is in there because of what *he* did.

You saved your children's lives."

"No, they saved mine!" she cries.

"I never would have left if it wasn't to protect *them*!

I didn't want them to be his prisoners too."

Prisoners?

Aren't prisoners behind bars because they did something bad?

Were we prisoners this whole time and Mama didn't tell us?

Daddy always said Mama did a lot of things wrong.

Did we do a lot of things wrong too?

DAYLIGHT

Mémère and Pépère's home is bright,
with big windows
that invite the outside in.
But in our bedroom,
Mama keeps pulling the shades down
even after I fling them up.
The darkness closes in on me,
making me feel trapped.
I shrink in the darkness,
smaller and smaller.
If we stay in this darkness forever,
we'll all shrink to nothing,
until we disappear.

HIS IDEA *of* FUN

I look out at the fields that surround the house.
A few small snow piles from the hard Maine winter
still linger in the valley.
Daddy loved taking us outside in the snow.
Mama was making dinner when the first flakes fell,
but she stopped to bundle us up so Daddy could take us out.
As soon as we stepped outside, he tossed Jenna up in the air.
She giggled.
He tossed her higher, and her face looked scared.
He tossed her even higher—
and waited to catch her till she fell lower—
and she started to cry.
I called out for him to stop.
"She's scared, Daddy! That's too high for her!"
"Too high? I'll show you high."
Mama ran out when she heard Jenna scream.
"What happened?" she said. "Is she hurt?"
Daddy's look told me not to say a word.
I stood there more frozen than the snow.
"She's just weak. You baby her," he snarled
as he walked away.

FREEDOM

Mémère's car feels like a magic carpet carrying us
through town, not like Daddy's rumbly diesel truck.
It's just the three of us going out this time,
and I see Mama smile for the first time in a while.
In the grocery store, Mama pushes the cart.
Daddy always did it *before*.
We walk down the ice cream aisle to the Popsicles,
and Mama lets us each pick our own box.
Jenna points to the rainbow-colored ones.
I choose peach, after staring at the flavors for a long time.
I'm not used to choosing.
Mama's not either—it takes her even longer
to decide on cookie dough ice cream.
We add more items to the cart, and each time, I hold my breath,
feeling like we're doing something wrong.
But I look around, and other people are doing it too—
they're choosing groceries just like us.
We walk down another aisle full of boxes with pretty pictures
on them.
"Let's get some tea," Mama says. "Maybe we can have tea
with Mémère and her friends sometime."
Mama's idea makes me happy, and we both smile as she
puts a box in the cart that has a pretty yellow lemon
painted on it.

STARINA

Mémère and Pépère and their neighbors and friends have
been giving us money to "help us get back on our feet."
Mama lays out all the paper dollars on the bed.
I've never seen so much. We never had our own money before.
It was always Daddy's money. But this time the money is ours,
and Mama knows just what we need—our own car—
so we can go anywhere we want, when we want.
We go with Pépère to look at a car for sale down the road.
The sides have rust, but it's mostly white and called an Explorer.
Pépère nods as he looks it over. Mama smiles and nods back.
"It'll help us explore the world—see things we haven't
been able to see yet," Mama whispers to me.
Things I didn't even know I was missing, I think.
I decide to name it Starina because the car
is bright like the stars,
and stars make me feel hopeful.

MOVING ON

This time, when we leave, we have enough time
to pack our stuff.
I'm packing my own things, and this should feel exciting,
but a sudden sadness pulls at me and I freeze.
I feel stuck, trapped, not sure what feels like home.
I'm afraid to stop moving for too long, so I find
some markers and write LACEY on my boxes
and draw flowers with crayons.
They're bluets, like the ones starting to bloom outside
that I've been drawing in my nature journal.
Then we fill Starina with so much stuff,
we can hardly see out the back windows.
Before we leave, Mémère hugs me.
She says, "We'll come visit you soon."
Pépère adds, "Enjoy the adventure."
They hand Mama a bouquet of flowers.
"For your new apartment," Mémère says,
"to bring the spring inside."
And then we're off.
Just the three of us, and Starina,
on our road to after.

PART TWO

Reaching
FOR THE
Sunlight

DOORS

Our new apartment
is at a place called Caring Unlimited—
a place for moms and kids like us
who also left their homes
because of abuse.
We walk up to the large gray building,
and a smiling lady
opens the glass door wide, inviting us inside.
"I'm Aubrey, your advocate," she says.
"I'm here to help if you need anything."
She explains that she'll visit us on Mondays, and I'm glad.
I like her smile and her fancy pins and her curly
silver-purple hair.
She leads us down a long hallway with lots of doors
and stops at the last door at the very end of the hall.
I get to turn the doorknob on the door that's ours.
There's a bright kitchen with a shiny floor,
not scuffed-up, splintery plywood like we had before,
and painted walls *with no holes punched out.*
Mama and Aubrey keep talking while
Jenna and I walk around, marveling at all
the doors to different rooms in our new apartment.
Before, only one room in our house had a door—
the upstairs bathroom, where we would hide
if we needed to get away from Daddy.

Sometimes he banged and banged on that door,
hollering for us to let him in.
My heart starts to thump, but I tell myself
it will be different here.
Here we can play hide-and-seek just for fun.
Here we can close doors gently just to find
a little quiet of our own.
Jenna and I do that now.
We find a small sunny room and sit down together,
watching sunbeams light up the floor.

COMMUNITY GARDEN

Before she leaves, Aubrey tells us about
a community garden that we're welcome to help with.
She says this afternoon,
other moms and kids who live here
will be planting flowers in the raised beds
in front of the parking lot.
My heart leaps. We have a garden here!
Yes, I want to plant. I want to grow flowers!
"Thank you," Mama says. "I'm not sure if we can."
"No pressure," Aubrey says. "It's your decision."
"Thank you," Mama repeats.
After she leaves, I beg Mama to let us help.
I tell her I want to see the flowers up close and
help plant them and add more to my journal.
She says the garden is too close to the road.
Someone from *his* family could drive by
and see us living here.
Later, I watch out the window as moms and kids
plant tall red flowers and bunches of small purple flowers.
I wish I knew what all of them were.
I wish I was the one with my hands in the dirt.

OUR BEDROOM

Mama moves the bunk beds from the kids' room
into her room
so we can all sleep in the same room together.
The top bunk will be mine.
Then she sets up a table in the kids' room
so she'll have a place to make art.
As we unpack, a photo of Daddy falls out of a book.
Daddy is holding me, and I'm wrapped in a yellow baby blanket.
Mama sees it and snatches it from my hands.
She places it in her things and says,
"Let's put this away for now."
I want to tell Mama that even though Daddy's in jail
and she doesn't want to see his picture,
I can still feel him in the corners of my mind,
telling me what I should say and do.
A bird sings outside my window,
and I envy her carefree song
because even though I'm free,
my thoughts are not.

THERAPISTS

Living at our new apartment means we'll have therapists.

It's part of the rules here.

Two women carrying clipboards knock on our door.

The taller one, with short brown hair, says,

"Hi, girls. I'm May, and this is Norah."

Norah has long, wavy black hair and a bag

full of—I peek—games!

She sees me looking and smiles, telling me we'll explore it later.

For now, we walk into the living room, and Norah sits

on the floor with us.

She asks us to imagine that

we are plants growing in the soil.

It doesn't sound exciting, but I try it and it's fun.

Jenna crouches into a ball, and I pretend to water her.

She slowly stands, uncurling her fingers,

reaching for the sun,

smiling.

NEW MORNING

Birds are singing
when I wake up the next morning.
Mama's still sleeping,
so I climb down from my top bunk
and peek around the curtain, into the day.
In the tree just outside our window, I see
a robin sitting on her nest.
Mama stirs in bed,
telling me to close the curtains,
so I grab my nature journal and let her and Jenna sleep.
I walk around the apartment, opening up all the curtains
Mama had closed.
It feels good to let the sunshine in.
I sit at the table and look outside.
The trees have buds,
and everything is coming back to life.
I sketch flowers, bushes, and birds
using my colored pencils in shades of soft peach,
fawn brown, and mossy green.
All I want to do is draw my new world
as I see it,
as I feel it.

HOMESCHOOL

May and Norah come over four days a week.
Mama says we're in a special program called HCT.
That stands for Home and Community Therapy.
It's for kids like us who have been through trauma.
They want to help me feel more comfortable in the world
and get Jenna to talk.
They tell Mama we need more of a schedule.
Mama explains how schedules feel like no freedom.
So there's a compromise: morning for school, afternoon for fun.
May says I'm lucky—
we have a lot more freedom than kids
in regular school.
"What's regular school?" I ask May as she places
some worksheets on the table.
I choose one about butterflies,
then she tells me about school.
It sounds hard to leave home every morning,
sit still, listen to teachers, and be surrounded
by kids and noise all day.
I'm glad I can stay home with Mama and Jenna,
like always.
Deep inside, though, my thoughts cloud over.
Mama has always been our schoolteacher,
so I thought that all moms were teachers
and all kids did school at home, like me.

Now I know I was wrong.

What else don't I know that I should?

I look down at my paper and realize

I misspelled *metamorphosis.*

I'm not used to worksheets like this.

Frustrated, I start to erase it,

but May gently stops me.

Then she gives me the biggest, brightest purple eraser

I've ever seen.

"Mistakes are more fun with this," she says.

"Go ahead and

 erase as much as you want."

CRAYONS

Norah knows how much Jenna and I like to draw, so she
brings us a new box of bright, beautiful crayons.
I open the box and
take a sniff, loving the waxy way they smell.
Jenna leans over and
grabs the box from my hands.
She smells them too, then nods, smiling.
She hands me a red crayon,
and I look at my blank paper.
I glide the crayon across the page and start drawing a line
that turns into a picture of
the dream I had last night,
where Starina was about to blow up.
The car's lights were blinking, and I flew in just in time
to save Jenna and Mama from the firestorm around us.
I don't know I'm crying until
a tear falls onto my drawing.
"Are you okay?" Norah asks.
"Can Daddy take our apartment and Starina?" I ask Mama.
"No," Mama says.
Her voice shakes in that one word.
No, I say in my head—
a word I never heard her say to Daddy.

"Can you tell us about your drawing?" May asks
in a kind voice.
At first, I don't want to talk about it, but
the look on their faces tells me it's okay.
I take a deep breath and tell them about my dream
even though it feels scary to say out loud.
"Thank you for sharing that with us," May says.
"I know it can be hard to say things out loud sometimes,"
Norah tells me.
"It gets easier, though," May says, patting me on the shoulder.
Mama comes over, and when she puts her arm around me,
I feel better.

PLAYGROUND

There's a playground nearby, and Mama finally
says we can go.
But first she hands us hats and sunglasses.
She says we must wear them whenever we leave
the apartment—
at least for now—
to make ourselves less recognizable.
Jenna tosses her hat to the ground,
but when I tell her we're playing dress-up,
she not only puts it back on but stacks a second hat on top.
Then she finds a necklace of beads in the toy box too.
When we get near the playground, Jenna points.
The pointy blue towers cut through the horizon.
We run ahead and discover a town of castles,
and the whole town is ours!
We climb up the middle section and claim the top nest.
Jenna laughs as we wave to Mama.
Later, I swing high,
passing through the sharp skyline,
then dip back down
to earth again.
Free.

SEPARATION

Mémère is here today
because Mama has to go to court.
May and Norah are here too.
It's the first time Mama has ever left without us.
My heart thumps and my throat feels stuck,
but I told her I would try to be brave,
for Jenna.
I don't know why I have to, though, because
Jenna doesn't want to try at all.
Her cries fill the apartment.
Mama's eyes say she doesn't want to go.
But Mama's voice says, "I love you. I'll be back soon."
I stand there, fists clenched,
and watch out our window as she leaves us.

TOGETHER

Even though we have bunk beds,
I sometimes sleep in Mama's bed
with her and Jenna.
Sometimes I feel like
I can't be without Mama.
I need to look over and know
she's there.
When she wraps me up
in a hug,
it's the only way
I feel safe.

BOOKS

Across the street from our new apartment, there's a library—
a place I've never visited before.
With our disguises on, we hold hands and cross quickly.
When we step inside the double glass doors, I'm amazed!
I've never seen so many books before.
The air smells sweet, and Mama says
it's the books—their old paper and ink.
I want to walk through each row and brush my hand
on each book.
I want to open them all and smell the pages
and read as many as I can.
At the desk, a nice man hands Mama
a plastic card with her name on it.
It makes a happy *ding!* sound when he scans it,
and that's all we need to do to borrow books for free.
Books about birds and flowers—
even field guides.
My pile is as tall as I can manage.
Next time,
I'll bring a big bag.

MEETING

Every Wednesday night at Caring Unlimited,
there is a meeting called Support Group
for mamas only—but Mama hasn't gone to one yet.
Aubrey told her she should try it
and that there's another room for the kids to play in.
"It's just down the hall," Aubrey said. "They'll be fine."
I wasn't so sure.
Tonight, Mama is going.
She takes us to the kids' room
and bends down to give us hugs.
"I'll come back in a little bit," she says, squeezing my hand.
My heart thumps.
Jenna stares where Mama was, her eyes
never leaving the spot where Mama just stood.
"Want to come play, girls?" a voice says.
We sit down at a table full of paper and crayons.
The whole time I try to gct Jenna to draw with me,
but she won't.
When Mama comes back,
her eyes are as teary as Jenna's.
Mama tells us, "I'm done with Support Group.
I'm *never* going back."

When we return to our apartment,
Mama gets out her

charcoal sticks and starts drawing trees.

Twisting trees, bending in the wind.

Without any words, she hands a piece of charcoal to me

and some crayons to Jenna,

and we all make tall, bendy trees together.

With each long line I draw,

another breath of sadness leaves me.

I breathe out,

letting it all go away,

and look over to see Mama is starting to relax too.

I wonder if talking about Daddy in the group got her upset.

Then I realize that right now is the first time

I've thought of Daddy this whole day.

Inside my head,

he's telling me what to do less and less,

and with each tree limb I draw,

I feel stronger.

EVERY SPACE IS FILLED

Every day here is full of people.
An endless trail of knocks and doorbells,
men and women coming over to talk to Mama.
About court. About Daddy.
About us.
I miss the quiet days alone, when it was us and Mama,
before Daddy got home.
Then the days were quiet
and the nights were loud.
Now it's the other way
around.
Today there's another new activity.
We start art lessons at a place called
River Tree Arts so we can
get used to being around other kids.
Mama sits in the room watching us,
making sure we're safe, she says.
She's the only parent that stays.
Jenna and I join a table, and I look around.
Other kids chatter and laugh together
so easily, it seems.
I'm not sure what to say, so instead
I just close my eyes for a minute
and feel the warmth
of the sunlight through the windows.

We each pick out a white piece of pottery—
ready for color, ready for paint.
I chose an open scallop-shaped seashell
so I can use it as a tray for beach treasures.
Jenna chooses a fish.
My paintbrush, dipped in robin's-egg blue,
touches the clay shell, soft like a whisper.
I make sure to cover all of it,
filling every space with paint.
"That's really good," the girl next to me says.
"Thanks," I say. "Yours is too."

SEED PICTURES

Norah comes over and says we can make flower pictures.
She lays out a huge pile of
seeds and beans on the table.
At first, I'm confused,
but then I see what she is doing.
Using drippy white glue,
she starts sticking seeds onto paper.
"Come on, want to make one? It's fun!" she says.
I make one with her, but it feels like a waste—
we should be eating or planting them.
"How did you like your first art class?" Norah asks.
"I painted a shell."
"Did you make any new friends?"
"One girl was nice," I say, but I don't tell her more
because the seeds and beans make my mind
fill with thoughts of *before*.
We never had so many beans before.
We didn't have grapes or apples or watermelon either.
Daddy yelled at Mama when she asked to buy fruit for us.
And he yelled at me when I asked to plant a garden.
"What kind is this pretty striped one?" I hold it up
to show Norah.
"A sunflower seed," she explains.
I save one in my pocket,
and after Norah leaves,

I grab a cup from the kitchen

and head outside.

Mama follows me out. "Lacey, what are you doing?"

"It'll just take a minute," I tell her.

Mama watches, with Jenna on her hip, as

I fill my cup with dirt

from the garden

I wish I was allowed to help in.

Then I tuck my sunflower seed into the soil.

Back inside, I sprinkle it

with a handful of water, like rain,

set it on the kitchen windowsill,

and wait.

A STONE'S THROW

Now that the weather's getting warmer,
Mama takes us to the beach some days.
We like to get there just as everyone else
is folding up their umbrellas to leave,
when the beach is just about empty.
Mama lets us explore while she reads on her towel.
We run.
We wade through the tide pools,
watching the hermit crabs travel.
I search for heart-shaped rocks but don't find any.
So instead, I pick up
as many smooth dark-gray stones
as I can find.
May told Mama that next time we go to the sea,
we could try throwing a rock
for each hurtful thing Daddy did,
but as I stop to pick more up, I think
there aren't enough stones on the beach for that.
After Daddy slammed the table,
saying he'd be my dentist, something changed.
Mama stopped crying, started making quiet phone calls.
Secret plans.
Mama kept them secret from me,
the same way she kept them from Daddy.
I wouldn't have told him.

I would've helped pack our things,
secretly, slowly.
I would have thought of a way to keep Mac.
I throw a rock as far as I can out into the waves
and watch it disappear.
Then I look down and see a rock
that's the perfect shape of a heart.
I turn it over in my hands, feeling
its smooth edges
and soft corners.
This one is coming home with me, and I won't have
to hide it under anything.

EVERYWHERE *and* NOWHERE

My stomach twists when Mama tells me
she has to go to court again.
But once I learn we can go with her this time,
and so can Mémère,
my stomach untwists just a little.
At the courthouse, we see Trooper Podos
and meet a lady from Child Protective Services
who says she'll be our caseworker and that she's on our side.
She brings us through a back door
into a white room
with a table and chairs,
stuffed animals, and games.
I'm surprised to find May and Norah are here too.
They stay with me and Jenna and Mémère
while Mama and our caseworker go upstairs to court.
May and Norah want to play games, but I can't focus.
I can't stop wondering if Daddy is up there.
If he knows we're here.

CONFLICTED

Sometimes Daddy's voice echoes in my mind.
You're nothing.
Nobody wants you.
I'm sorry she is your mother.
Hearing it makes me doubt myself,
and sometimes it makes me doubt Mama.
Sometimes I don't know what to think.
Daddy went to jail because Mama told the police.
If she never told on him,
we would all still be together,
with Mac.
Sometimes this makes me really angry.

PUNCHING BAG

Mama gets us a punching bag,
and we help set it up in the apartment.
We put on big black gloves, and I punch it
and kick it and punch it again.
I think of Daddy and all the words he said,
all the times he hurt Mac,
scared Jenna, made fun of Mama.
Maybe Mama thinks of that, too, when she's punching.
Neither of us stops punching until we're both out of breath.
Jenna stands back, watching.
I didn't know I could hit that hard.
I didn't know I wanted
to hit something that hard.

BRANCHING OUT

Jenna still sleeps with Mama, so
I have the bunk beds to myself.
Now I'm ready for a whole room to myself.
I ask Mama if we can move the bunks back.
"Are you sure?" she asks.
"I want to try," I say.
So for one night,
before we move the bunks back,
we set up a bed made of couch cushions
on the floor of the other bedroom.
I bring my cup with my seed into my room
and set it on the windowsill so
the morning sun can shine on it.
The seed needs the sun to sprout.
I lie on my floor bed
while Jenna and Mama sleep
in the room next to me, with our doors open,
thinking how peaceful our new apartment is.
Once or twice in the night I notice
Mama checks on me,
but I am fine in my room all night
until the sun kisses the windowsill, and my seed,
good morning.
The next day, we move the bunks for good,
and Mama moves her art table

out of my bedroom
to a corner of the living room,
near her tree paintings.
They're leaning against the apartment wall
like rows of trees lining the side of the road,
only these trees are different.
They're twisting,
reaching,
searching
for something—
maybe sun,
maybe light,
maybe freedom.

SANCTUARY

I read about Rachel Carson in one of my library books
and find out one of her wildlife sanctuaries is nearby.
Mama takes us for a hike there, and along the trail
there are lookout points with wooden decks
numbered 1 through 12.
I make sure to look out at the marshes from each one.
I have my nature journal and binoculars,
so I make a list and sketch some of the birds we see.
Mama knows them all and tells me their names.
Canada Geese,
Mallard Ducks,
Great Blue Herons,
and a Snowy Egret.
She said Pépère taught her about birds
when they used to go for walks in the woods.
I'm starting to know some bird names
now that I can be outside with them,
watching them, listening to their songs,
seeing their great big world.
The more we walk outside and explore,
the more I know my world is getting bigger too.

A NEW NOW

Mama and I are baking today while Jenna takes a nap.

I put on my apron—the one Mémère made for Mama years ago.

When I wear it, I like to imagine Mama

when she was a kid,

when she was happy.

Before Daddy made things hard for her.

Mama sets a big bowl

and the brownie mix on the counter.

I crack the eggs, add oil and water.

Mama shows me how to use the mixer.

While the brownies are baking, I ask,

"Mama, how much water should I give a seed?"

"Seeds are delicate things," she says.

"Not enough water dries a seed out,

but too much, and it can't grow.

If you give a seed a little misting of water

each day, a few hours of sunlight,

and enough love and time, it will grow."

I consider this.

Maybe I've been giving mine too much water.

"I might have a spray bottle you can use," she adds.

Mama takes the brownies out of the oven to cool

in one smooth motion, and it hits me:

She makes food differently now.

She bakes what she wants to when she wants to.

Right now in this kitchen,

this bright and cheerful kitchen,

she looks happy.

Later, while we're enjoying our gooey brownies,

Mama tells us that

she got accepted to

a graduate school in Virginia called Hollins.

Caring Unlimited is helping her find

assistance and scholarships,

and the school offers financial aid.

Her six-week summer semester starts next month, in June—

Mama must see my nervousness, because she adds,

"We're going to just try it out."

Jenna is having fun smooshing her brownie.

"I've always dreamed of illustrating children's books,

and this will help me do that."

As she talks, I realize a few things.

We've never left Maine before.

"It will help us," she says.

I never knew my mom had dreams before.

There was so much we couldn't do *before*

because of Daddy.

There's so much we can do now,

but I wonder if I'm ready.

HAIRCUTS

Before we leave for Virginia, we get our first real haircuts.

Mémère is a hairstylist, so we visit her salon.

I hop up onto one of the fancy chairs, and Mémère smiles,

swooshing a cape around my neck

that covers me from neck to toes.

Mémère spins the chair around, and

I see us in the mirror now.

I think of how much we look like family.

She holds the shiny gold scissors in her hand,

and immediately my brain remembers what haircuts

used to be like.

Daddy used to cut our hair.

Mama always stood to the side, hands fidgeting.

Scissors snipped, clipped at my hair,

strands falling straight to the floor,

sharp blades whispering near my ears, eyes, and neck.

I tried not to flinch.

After, I would peek in the mirror

and want to cry but never dared to.

This haircut feels different.

Mémère is humming, and Mama and

I like the way my hair looks.

Jenna hops up next, no problem.

ROAD TRIP

We pack our bags and fill Starina to the brim again,
ready for our road trip to Virginia.
We stop at Mémère and Pépère's to say bye for the summer.
Standing in the field for a picture with them,
the camera clicks, and suddenly, tears fall.
Maybe I'm a little bit scared to leave.
Mémère understands, and wraps her arms around me.
Pépère picks a bright purple flower
from their clematis vine
and hands it to me.
He shows me how the petals reach out
like a star with lots of points,
a small yellow firework bursting in the center.
One flower, so complex
for such a tiny thing,
showing me it's okay for things not to be simple.
The road to Virginia
stretches out for miles ahead of us.
Soft music fills the car while
I draw flowers in my journal.
First, the clematis, then
buttercups and blue flag irises.
I recognize so many flowers from nature now because of
the field guides I borrowed from the library.

What I'm hoping to see most of all in Virginia
is a magnolia tree.
By tonight we'll be in Pennsylvania.
It will be our first time sleeping at a hotel.
We cruise through curves and
coast through the valleys.
The best view is up in the mountains.
I find the right shade of
green colored pencil and draw
the mountain so I'll always have it with me.
My ears pop as we drive uphill,
close to the wispy clouds.
So close I feel I could reach out and touch them,
like I'm on top of the world.

LOCKED IN *for the* NIGHT

We check in to the motel in Pennsylvania,
and the clerk gives us
our very own key to our own room.
Mama walks us to the room and tells us to stay put
as she rushes to and from the car, bringing our things in,
shutting the door tight each time.
It's dark and damp and small,
like before,
but it's only for one night, I tell myself.
Jenna sees a notepad and pen on a desk and draws
her teddy bear,
so I find it in the bags for her.
Once Mama's finished, she closes the curtains,
triple-checks the locks,
and says, "We're safe inside.
No one goes outside."

HONEYBEES

The next day, I'm excited to be on the road again.
I've decided I like car trips.
Looking out the window at green mountains, blue skies,
and sunshine fills me with sweetness and warmth—
maybe this is what hope feels like?
We pass several large trucks in a row, and all of a sudden—bees!
So many bees flying with us, outside the windows.
Mama sees them, too, and says there must
be a beekeeping truck nearby.
By the look on Jenna's face, I can tell that she's scared,
she was stung before,
so I tell her, "It's okay. They're outside."
More bees keep buzzing by, swarming as we drive,
and one sticks himself to my window,
holding on tight,
hanging on for miles.
I watch him closely—noticing his big eyes,
fuzzy body, and tiny feet gripping on to the glass.
Finally, after miles and miles, one leg lifts off,
and the bee lets go
and is gone.
Then rain hits us hard,
like a waterfall on the windshield.
The bee knew it was the exact right time
to let go.

SUMMER HOUSE

After two days of driving, we pull onto a street
called Bluemont Avenue and stop in front of a brick house.
Chairs that look like they're woven from baskets
sit on a porch the full length of the house.
"Is this where we're staying?" I ask.
"Yup," Mama says.
"The whole house?" I ask.
"All of it," she replies.
"Welcome to our summer home."
I take it all in.
How will it feel to have so much space?
Two stories. A front porch.
Mama turns the key, *click*,
and we walk inside.
The polished wood floors gleam like golden honey
from the sunlight streaming
through the windows.
But not for long, because Mama
hurries to pull down the blinds.
"Mama," I protest as
the room gets darker.
"You never know who's looking in," she says.
As if *he* followed us to Virginia.
Will we always have to worry about *him*?

The house is hot and stuffy with the windows closed,
and it smells like earth, with a bit of dog.
I look around and spot
a tuft of dog hair on the floor,
reminding me of Mac.
My heart pangs for him.
Upstairs there are two bedrooms.
Since Jenna still sleeps with Mama,
I get a room all to myself!
Once my own door is closed,
I pull up the blinds.
Even if someone was out there,
they can't peek in on the second floor.
I feel like I'm in my own secret tower.
When I set my sunflower on the windowsill—
I notice it has sprouted!
Its tiny green leaves reach out
for the sun.

MIDDLE GROUND

In the space between here
and the house next door,
there's a shady garden
with stepping-stones
and a swing that sways
from a tree
full of pale-pink blossoms.
I listen to the cardinal singing above
and watch robins hopping below.
I want to hop too—
across the stepping-stones
in the space between here
and there.

CICADAS

The hot Virginia air sticks to my skin.
A constant buzzing fills my ears—
giant bugs called cicadas play a symphony every day,
announcing it's over eighty-two degrees.
I know this because we had them in Maine too—
only they didn't sing as often because
it wasn't always this hot.
When I find some of their old exoskeletons,
I put them in a glass jar.
I love how cicadas outgrow themselves
and become something new.
Something different
than they were *before*.
Maybe I can shed my old life
like an exoskeleton too?

NO CHOICE

Mama hired a lady named Miss Evie
to watch us
while she goes to her classes.
We've never stayed with anyone else,
except for Mémère and Pépère.
Jenna cries the whole way there.
I know how she feels, but
I don't let myself cry right now.
What if Mama can't come back?
What if someone takes her away and we're not
there to help?
What if Daddy finds us here?

When we arrive, Miss Evie's house looks pretty.
Her yard is shaded by pine trees, and
there's a pink kiddie pool on the front lawn.
I point it out to Jenna, but
she ignores me
and clings to Mama, leaving marks on her skin.
Miss Evie comes out, extends her arms, and says,
"Here, just give her to me. She'll be fine."
Mama starts to pass her to Miss Evie, but
Jenna won't let go and starts to howl.
The other kids come over to stare.

Jenna won't talk, but
she *can* scream.
She screams and screams, and now I'd like to too—
or at least disappear.
Finally, Mama says, "I can't do this. Sorry."
Miss Evie looks upset as we
leave her pretty pine-shaded yard.
We pile back into Starina, and
Mama says she'll have
to take us to school with her.
She has no choice.

NOT ALLOWED

As we turn into Mama's school,
I spot a creek I want to play in, but
Mama says another time.
We're running late.
We park and hurry to her class, walking fast.
When Mama's professor sees us, she looks confused.
She steps out into the hall with us and tells Mama
that she can't bring children to class.
That we'll be a distraction.
This is a graduate school, not a place for kids.
Mama looks down, apologizes.
We walk back down the hall and sit in a stairway.
"I just have to think for a minute," Mama says,
and she buries her face in her hands.
I'm not sure what to do, but I sit down too
and hold Jenna on my lap for her.
I think I hear Mama sniffle, but when she looks up,
her eyes stare ahead and she says, "Let's go."
I carry Jenna all the way to the car and
point out birds to her on the drive
back to Bluemont Avenue.

The VIEW

The next day, Mama tells us she's arranged
for another student to watch us
in a room down the hall from
her classroom.
It's important, Mama says,
that we're okay with this.
We will just be without her
for a little while.
Jenna's lip starts to quiver, and
I reach for her hand
while we follow Mama to the room.
"We'll be okay. Mama will be real close by," I whisper to Jenna,
hoping to reassure her—
and myself.
When we meet the student, Marcia, I like her right away.
Her kind eyes sparkle at us, and
she talks to me like
I'm a grown-up.
The room is bright, with
windows all around.
This *will* be all right, after all.
Mama starts to leave, but
Jenna pulls at her and starts to cry.
Mama tries to calm Jenna, repeating she won't be far.

She gives us each a hug and
tries to head toward the door,
but Jenna hangs on to her leg and
starts screaming.
Mama tries to pry Jenna off.
"Lacey," pleads Mama, "help me!"
But I'm frozen stuck where I stand
and don't know what to do.
Marcia watches; she seems frozen too.
Mama stops trying and collapses on the floor,
picking Jenna up,
holding her close.
Mama hides her face in Jenna,
but I can feel her defeat.

WHAT NOW?

Another woman walks in,
says she's sorry,
but we have to leave.
Our noise level is disturbing
other students in the building.
Mama says she's sorry. So sorry.
She just thought,
just hoped this would work.
"Please give me time to work something out,"
Mama says to the lady.
"The last day to drop classes is Monday," she says.
"You have until then."
"Thank you," says Mama.
I was hoping this wouldn't be
so hard for Jenna.
I hadn't realized how hard it would be
for all of us.

SECRET

When I think of being without Mama,
I feel cold,
unsure,
off balance,
confused.
A memory of Daddy invades my thoughts.
He knelt down in front of me, taking my hand.
"Lacey, you're gonna have to get used to a life without Mama."
I held my breath. What did he mean?
His eyes so still and calm, a smile almost forming.
A hint I was supposed to get.
Mama came up the basement steps with laundry.
Our eyes met and hers filled with fear.
I stood quietly, afraid to move.
Daddy said some things to us that will never go away.

FINALLY, the CREEK

Since we don't have to be
anywhere now, Mama lets me
wade in the creek while
she and Jenna sit on the grassy bank.
I try to get Jenna to join me, but
she just wants Mama.
The creek is cool and shady.
Enormous heart-shaped leaves dangle
from the trees above.
As the sun shines through, it speckles the ground
in a pretty lacelike pattern.
Lacey—just like my name.
Wading in the water is
as wonderful as I hoped it would be.
Minnows swim around my feet.
A crawfish blends in with the rocks.
She doesn't know I see her, but I do.
Then I see a real snake!
"Snake!" I say. "Come see!"
But Mama is not as happy about it as I am.
"Get out, Lacey!" she shouts, so I jump out of the water,
up onto the grass, and watch the snake from above.
It's so graceful as it slithers away.
I sit on the grass next to Mama and Jenna

and make a quick sketch in my nature journal
so next time we're at the library
I can look up what kind of snake it was,
if it's venomous or not.
After I draw, I look out at the creek.
The water flows into the woods,
making its own
winding road,
like a scribble,
through the land,
until I can't see it anymore.
"Mama, the creek is so twisty," I say.
"Water never finds its way in a straight line," she says.
Then she adds, "It always finds a way through.
No matter the obstacles,
it keeps flowing."

SAVING the DAY

Mémère is coming to save the day!
That's Mama's new plan.
We arrive at the airport early
to watch planes coming and going.
Everyone here is moving so quickly.
They all have places to be.
For the first time, I feel like I am part of a wide world.
While we wait, I make up stories
about their lives, their trips, their homes.
Then Mama says, "I think that's her plane, girls!"
We all start to cry when we see Mémère, but it's a happy cry.
Mémère approaches and gives Jenna and me each
a flowery gift bag with shiny tissue paper.
I lift something out of mine, and it's a doll!
I've never had a doll before.
She has a blue dress, soft sewn legs and arms,
and brown yarn for hair.
Jenna's doll looks like mine, but hers has a pink dress.
She's never had a doll before either.
Jenna holds it up and gives Mémère the biggest smile,
lighting up the whole airport.

LOVE

On Monday morning,
Mémère stands with us on the
porch so we can wave goodbye to Mama.
"I love you," Mama says.
"Love you too," I say, and Jenna points
to the heart on her teddy bear,
then points to her own.
Mama gets into Starina without us and
drives away, waving.
Jenna whimpers, and
I tighten my fists at my sides,
but Mémère takes our hands and reminds us,
"She will be back, girls."
In the house,
Jenna and I settle on the floor to draw.
I make her a funny chicken because
I know she likes them.
Jenna picks up a crayon too
and draws a wobbly chicken next to mine.
"Bawk bawk," I squawk,
and Jenna lets out
a small giggle.
Since Jenna is happy sitting with Mémère,
I head upstairs to water my sunflower.

There's a tiny prickly bud
forming on the top of the stem!
The green outside layers
are folded into itself tight.
It is making petals inside.
Soon it will be ready to bloom.
Maybe Mama, Jenna, and I
are like my sunflower,
full of changes going on inside
that others can't see,
good changes,
even if
they might feel prickly
at first.

MEETING HALFWAY

Mémère is making us breakfast when
I look out the window
and see a boy walk over to the tree swing.
He swings alone until someone shouts,
"Eric, pancakes!"
"Be right there, Dad!" the boy replies.
Before he leaves, he notices me at the window
and waves.
His father's voice sounds so different
from my own daddy's voice,
which always boomed like thunder.
Later, there are two kids out near the swing—
Eric again, and a girl.
Mémère suggests I say hi,
so I walk down our porch steps
into the space between our houses.
They look up at me, and I
nervously shuffle my feet in the grass.
"Hey," Eric says. "What's your name?"
"Lacey," I mumble.
"I'm Lesley," the girl standing near him says. "That's Eric."
"I'm eleven," says Eric, "and Lesley is ten. How old are you?"
"Same as you," I say.
I notice Lesley's neat ponytail, striped shirt, and khaki shorts.

Eric has a short haircut and glasses
and wears a white polo shirt,
khaki shorts, and shiny shoes.
I look down at my old, faded sundress and
worn-out flip-flops.
"Kiddos," their mom calls from their porch. "Time to go!"
"We have to leave," Lesley says,
"but you can use our swing whenever."
I watch them get into their shiny silver minivan with
their mom, dad, and baby sister.
They seem so different from my family,
like they're from another world,
and it makes me wonder how many worlds there are
and where I might fit in.

HOLLINS MAGIC

Mémère suggests we go with Mama
to campus for the day, for a change.
We can't join Mama inside the studio,
but her art professor says we can make our own art
with Mémère outside on the Hollins walking paths.
So while Mama gets to work, we do too,
drawing patterns on the walkways,
decorating them with things that we love.
I stand back and admire our art.
A student walks by and says, "Nice butterflies and books!"
I smile at her and say, "Thank you."
"I wish the whole campus was that colorful," she adds
before continuing on her way.
Then Mémère shows us how to make hopscotch grids—
a game where you hop,
with one foot or two,
sometimes skipping numbers.
I'm skipping on the grid when I get to the end and look up.
I don't know how I didn't see it before—
a tree with the biggest, brightest flowers I've ever seen!
Blossoms as big as a dinner plate!
Right then, I know this must be a magnolia.
Mémère and Jenna catch up to me, and we ooh and aah.
I breathe in its sweet and spicy scent,
and then I get my nature journal and start sketching.

Later, when we're too hot outside, we move inside and
play a quiet game of hide-and-seek in the Hollins library.
It's our version because I make sure Jenna's never alone
and Mémère can always spot us from her reading nook.
We crouch behind a cardboard Raggedy Ann,
between bookshelves, under tables.
Jenna shuffles from spot to spot, giggling.
Back outside, we have a picnic, and Mémère teaches us
how to make flower crowns using daisies and clovers,
while bunnies play their own game of hide-and-seek
across the lawn and under shrubs.
I lie next to Mémère on a blanket, staring at the sky,
and realize we can be okay without Mama sometimes.

BUGS

In the evening, we sit on the porch with Mémère
while Mama does homework inside.
Hundreds of moths try to get in the house
anytime I open the door because they like
the bright porch light.
We hear a June bug crash into the house.
Jenna runs to it, sees it kicking on its back.
She picks it up and holds it up to the night sky,
presenting the June bug to the universe,
and it flies away.
Sometimes
I love how pieces of this big world
can be so wonderful and small
at the same time.

RETREAT

Sometimes the hours while Mama is away at school
last longer than my ideas of what to do.
Some days I don't feel like drawing with sidewalk chalk,
or blowing bubbles, or reading,
or sketching in my nature journal,
or playing animals with Jenna.
I don't even feel like making brownies
or doing anything else on my list of things
I couldn't do before.
Lesley and Eric are at camp most of the day,
but one rainy afternoon they invite me over.
Mémère calls Mama, who says no, I can't go.
That she doesn't know them enough.
She always says no, and I feel like I'm stuck all over again.
I wish the punching bag was here with us!
Sometimes all I want to do
is hide up in my room and cry.
Sometimes, in its own way,
it feels good to cry.

COMMON GROUND

Lesley is outside my window
on Saturday morning,
waving at me to join her, and
Mama says okay this time,
but I have to stay in the yard.
"Hey," Lesley says in greeting. "It's sure hot today, isn't it?"
I nod. Not sure what else to say.
Lesley starts jumping on
the stepping-stones in the garden,
and I follow.
Eric watches us from the swing.
"Be careful," Lesley tells me. "There's hot lava below."
"It makes the stones *so* hot you have to move fast," I add,
playing along with the game
and happy to be hopping
on these honeycomb-shaped stones.
"Right!" she says. "Don't get burned!"
Eric laughs at us as we hop to the end,
not slipping into the lava, and then hop back again.
"Why doesn't your sister talk?" Lesley asks.
"She just doesn't," I say.
"Why doesn't your mom let you come over to our house?"
she asks.
"Where's your dad?" Eric asks.

All these questions.

I breathe in, try to speak,

but only silence comes out.

The lava under my feet feels real now.

It's a bird that rescues me—

a bright-red Northern Cardinal

singing loudly from the trees above us.

We all lie down in the grass to listen.

"Did you know they're Virginia's state bird?" Lesley asks.

"I just love watching them," Eric says.

"Me too," I say.

Finally, in the space between

our two houses

we find common ground.

NOTICING

The days without Mama fly by like the cardinals
through the trees.
One day I notice that I don't mind anymore
when Mama has to leave.
I notice that I feel okay, even as she is driving away,
because I know she comes back each time.
I notice that Jenna's getting better at it too and
doesn't cry or yell anymore.
I notice that Mama doesn't come back to the door
several times before she actually leaves.
I notice that the cicadas are singing every day
and my sunflower is starting to unfold its tiny petals!
It's getting too tall for its cup.

A WORLD of BOOKS

Mémère takes us to the public library and lets us
choose piles and piles of books and videos.
I find books about cats, gardens, and making art.
My favorite picture book so far is *Miss Rumphius*,
about a lady who loved flowers too
and planted them everywhere.
Before, we could never have books.
Before, we could never watch movies when Daddy wasn't home.
He knew exactly where he pressed pause
before he turned the TV off,
so if we or Mama turned it back on,
he could tell, and we'd be in trouble.
Back at the house,
it feels good to be able to leave our books out on the table,
to play a movie whenever and for however long we want.

ROOM *for* GROWTH

One morning, I find my sunflower
tipped over on its side, the dirt spilled out.
I use my hands to scoop up the dirt,
push it back down into the cup, and
prop it up against the wall.
I know it's not a permanent solution.
When I show Mémère how tall my sunflower's grown,
she says it's time to plant it outside,
that it will eventually be taller than me.
My heart sinks.
I hadn't realized it would grow so big,
that I wouldn't always be able to keep it with me.
But I nod, knowing it's what my flower needs.
We walk into the yard and find a pretty spot
against the brick wall of this Bluemont Avenue house
where it will stay here in Virginia,
even if we don't.

OUTSIDE

The heat today is cicadas-singing-at-full-volume hot.
In the afternoon, Lesley and Eric invite us over to play
in their sprinkler.
Lesley turns the faucet on, sending ribbons of cool water out
in spinning spirals for us to jump over.
The coldness catches me by surprise,
but it feels so good in the heat!
So this is what skipping around
in a sprinkler
with friends
feels like.

WATER WAYS

Mama comes home late at night.
While we're having dinner together,
she tells us about her class, her homework,
and I tell her about the sprinkler
and how much fun we had.
As I'm describing the water to her,
I remember the creek water too.
Water bends,
water flows,
water goes where it needs to go.
Mama, Jenna, and me—
we are like water
finding our way.

PAINTING FACES

One day, Lesley brings out her face paints.

She says I should be a tiger, and Jenna a cat,

and Eric wants to be a bear.

"I'll do the painting," Lesley says, "because they're my paints."

I'm not about to argue.

She draws a whisker. It tickles.

"So, where's your dad?" Lesley asks. "You never answered."

"In jail," I say.

"Why? What did he do?"

When I don't answer, she says, leaning in,

"My dad wouldn't do anything to have to go to jail."

"Yeah," Eric agrees. "So why's he in jail?"

"It's hard to explain," I finally say. "He wouldn't let us leave."

"Leave where?" Lesley asks as she colors my nose.

"Our house," I say, trying not to sneeze.

"Who couldn't even leave their own house?" Eric asks.

"Yeah, that makes no sense," Lesley agrees.

"You must be lying."

Suddenly I feel as small as the buzzing cicadas.

I want to hide up in the trees with them.

I start to leave, but just then, Mémère appears.

She wants to takes pictures of us in our face paint.

"Smile!" she says.

But I don't feel like smiling anymore.

ROCK WALL

They cannot call me a liar
like Daddy used to call Mama.
Liar.
That word. That sting.
I decide I don't even need friends
if that's what friends do.
I'll never talk to them again.
My world feels like it's closing in.
Daddy always said he was the wall
protecting us from the dangerous world.
Maybe he was right.
Maybe we needed the wall.
Maybe the world is as awful as he said it was
and we needed to stay home,
hidden from it all.

RAGE

Lesley and Eric play in the space between, laughing—
but now I only go out there when they're not home.
My nature journal is all the company I need,
that and the field guides Mémère got me.
I'm happy drawing alone in the cool air-conditioning.
I could draw from field guides for days,
except Jenna's always taking my things.
How can I draw my sunflower if she's stolen my yellow marker?
I go and grab it back from her, and I don't even care
that I make her cry.
If she wants to borrow it again, she can ask for it—with words.

POP'S

I'm looking at the National Audubon Society's
Field Guide to North American Wildflowers
when Mémère says, "Let's go somewhere."
She walks us over to Pop's Ice Cream,
and it's the best place.
The servers wear paper hats, and they have every kind of
ice cream treat you could ever imagine.
I feel strange being here without Mama,
especially since she loves ice cream too.
A wave of guilt washes over me for having fun without her,
but we're doing lots of things differently now than *before*,
and I know she would say it's okay,
so I try to be brave.
Jenna's pink ice cream soda arrives with a paper lace doily
under the glass and a long spoon and straw in it.
She claps when it's placed in front of her.
Mémère gets a chocolate cone,
and my two scoops of lemon crunch are served
in a fancy silver dish, with another doily underneath.
When I try it, the lemony candy melts in my mouth.
It's so delicious that it makes it a little easier to not
worry about Mama,
or anything else, for a moment.

FINALLY

After the six weeks are up,

Mama's summer term is done.

Mémère has already flown home,

so we help Mama clean the house on Bluemont Avenue.

And we go with her to Hollins to help her move out

of her art studio.

We load a cart up with Mama's supplies—

paints, brushes, inks, and colored pencils—

and some of the artwork she made.

I like all of her paintings, but I love the one

of a girl who looks like me the best.

She wears a blue cape and she's in a garden,

holding a basket of morning glories.

Mama creates such beautiful things.

I want to be able to do that too.

I want to make stuff people will enjoy,

like when I drew on the pathways with chalk

for the students walking by.

Before we leave, we take a picture of us in front

of the art building.

I look back as we drive out of Hollins University for the last time.

The winding creek reminds me that things will be okay.

If water can make its own way,

so can I.

SUNSET

Swinging outside
alone in the sweet summer air
on our last night in Virginia,
I start thinking about how
Daddy is not the wall around us anymore.
For the first time I know what it's like
to live without walls blocking me in,
and even though it feels harder sometimes,
I like it way better.
The sky glows as the sun falls,
and I swing a little higher
to catch the last light.

LEAVING AGAIN

With Starina packed, we're ready to make the trip
back to Maine.
We check the house one last time so that we aren't
forgetting anything.
Mama checks two last times.
Before we leave, I say goodbye to my sunflower—
and I get an idea.
Feeling for the biggest seeds
on the edge of the flower's center, I twist a few out.
They're smaller and softer and less striped than my first seed,
but I'll plant them next summer at our new home in Maine
so I can keep a little bit of my first flower with me.
Lesley is on the swing when I walk out front,
and Eric comes outside too.
I stand there like I did on the day we met.
"Well, bye, I guess," Eric says first.
"We mostly had fun," Lesley adds.
"Yeah, thanks," I say.
We get into Starina, and as Mama drives away,
I turn my seeds over in my hand.
We did have some fun here.
Hollins has been like our own garden,
a place where we could grow.

PART THREE

Blooming

ARRIVING HOME

This drive is like the other drive,
except this one is more about arriving—
arriving at our new home.
It's white but its roof and shutters are green,
the color of spring.
A big picture window overlooks our yard, where
there's space for a big garden.
But the best thing about our new house is
it's across the street from Mémère and Pépère,
who are waiting for us when we arrive.
The other best thing is my bedroom.
Pépère painted it the pale-yellow color I picked out,
and it has its own built-in bookshelves.
I unpack all my books before anything else,
which makes it feel like a library,
like I'm finally home.

I FIND MY SPACE

I wake up early, before anyone else,
on the first morning in our new home.
I go to the living room, open the curtains,
and curl up on the couch
under a soft gray blanket.
In this moment alone,
our home is all mine.
The amber sunlight introduces itself,
and I say hello back.

KITTENS

Mama has a surprise for us.
We're getting kittens!
She says we can each choose one
at the animal shelter.
When we arrive at Second Chances,
the air smells like cats and dogs.
We're greeted by a worker,
who leads us through a door with a cat silhouette.
We walk down a hallway
lined with cats and kittens
behind windows on both sides.
The kittens all look so sweet, it's hard to choose.
But near the far corner of the last window,
there are two kittens snuggling together—
the worker points them out
and says they are brothers.
One is all black with yellow eyes.
One is black and white with green eyes.
When Jenna and I press our faces to the glass,
the kittens come up to the other side of it.
The worker asks if we want to meet them.
We smile and nod.
With a click of the door,
the black-and-white kitten skips out first, fast,

up and down the hall, then

stops to rub up against my leg.

The other kitten peeks out of the door shyly

with his bright, round eyes.

Jenna scoops him up,

and he buries his nose in her neck.

They are perfect for us.

MITTENS and MARBLE

At home, we set up the kittens with all that they need.
My kitten's black-and-white fur reminds me of Mac.
I sit there watching him, trying to think of a name.
He takes small steps with white paws that look like mittens—
Mittens, we'll call him.
Next I watch the all-black kitten.
His eyes are big as he surveys his new home.
They shine bright like yellow glass.
Marble, we'll call him.
They wander cautiously
around us and the furniture,
then finally settle down together,
cuddling on the footstool.
Jenna and I sit across from them.
Two pairs, both bonded from the start.

NEIGHBORS

The doorbell rings the next day.
Since Mama still won't let me answer the door,
I watch her open it to a tall woman
with dark hair twisted high on her head
and a girl about my age.
They give Mama a loaf of banana bread,
and she calls me to join them.
I'm holding Mittens, and the girl reaches out to pet him.
"He's so fluffy!" she says. "I'm Brooke."
"Yeah." I smile.
"We just got him and his brother. I'm Lacey."
Brooke comes inside and watches Jenna flop Marble
from her lap
onto the living room floor.
Marble rolls over, showing off his belly, and we laugh.
We play with the kittens until Brooke's mom says it's time to go.
"We'd love to have Lacey over sometime," she adds.
Mama agrees, surprising me, while Brooke says, "Yay, soon!"
Back in my room, I snuggle with Mittens and
feel a small seed of hope growing in me.
Mittens purrs and plays a game with my bedspread,
batting at it like a pro boxer.
I think he likes it here.
I do too.

PIECE *by* PIECE

On Saturday, Pépère pulls into our driveway with
his pickup truck.
The back is filled with planks of wood and stuff.
"Girls!" he calls out. "We have something for you!"
Mama winks at me as we walk outside,
like she's in on what's happening.
As Pépère and some of his friends start unloading
pieces onto the lawn, I'm trying to imagine them together.
Then I see something that looks like a slide.
It's a swing set!
We never had our own playground before.
Brooke comes over, and we help them put it together.
There's not only a slide
but also monkey bars, three swings,
and a canopy cloth for the top deck.
When they are done,
we give Pépère a big hug and thank him
and his friends too.
Mama plays with Jenna on the slide
while Brooke and I swing.
We're quiet at first, not sure what to say,
but it feels okay.
Then Brooke has an idea.
"We should make a garden together," she says.

"In the space between our two houses."

She points to an open sunny spot.

"See where that milkweed is growing? Near there!"

"Yes! Let's do that," I say, and

just then, a monarch flies past.

"Ooh, so pretty," Brooke says. "We'll leave the milkweed

for monarchs."

"Right!" I nod. "They'll be migrating soon."

Brooke and I smile as

we swing opposite each other.

I go back,

she goes forward,

alternating in a pattern.

I'm happy she cares about monarchs

and is so easy to be with.

I look up at our new home,

feeling thankful.

Kittens.

Swing set.

And a plan for a garden we'll grow

in the space between

our two houses.

The PROBLEM with FRESH PAINT

Every time I walk into my room, I love seeing
the fresh yellow paint, like sunlight, on my walls.
But sometimes, it stings.
It reminds me that this whole house
is different from our house *before*.
Daddy didn't want us having
nice things,
finished things.
Maybe I don't deserve them.
It's hard to shake the sadness when it grips me.
It's the kind of sadness that feels bigger than the world
but makes you feel smaller than a grain of sand.
What I make myself do is take one step, then another.
I find my nature journal and draw anything—
like the American Goldfinch that hangs out at our feeders.
I focus on drawing the bird's bright-yellow body
and black-and-white wings.
Mittens gets jealous when I draw.
He jumps up and plops himself down on my work,
purring and demanding attention.
I pet him and love how soft he is.
His purring helps pull the sadness away too.

MIXED FEELINGS

Those things that Daddy said
and did *before*
live inside my memory.
Sometimes they move into the spaces of now,
and I never know when to expect them.
Sometimes I stop and stare
and realize that Daddy's voice
will never say new things to us again.
And I don't always know
how I feel about that.
Mama says I'll be able to talk to our new therapist
about all this.
We won't have May and Norah here because
moving away from Caring Unlimited means we don't
have daily in-home therapy.
We'll start seeing a new therapist soon,
once a week, at their office.
I think I will have a lot to ask them.

IRISES

We're playing outside when Mémère and her friend Sharron
come by carrying big, open-top cardboard boxes full of
what looks like dirt at first, until they get closer,
and I see it's—
bulbs!
"We brought you iris bulbs to help start your garden,"
Mémère says.
"If you plant them now they'll bloom in the spring."
"We have to wait until spring?" I ask.
"Some things just need to take their own sweet time,
 but when they arrive
you'll see they're worth the wait," Mémère explains.
"We collected bulbs from each of our gardens," Sharron adds.
"You're going to have plenty of variety—it'll be glorious!"
Brooke and I say thank you over and over.
"Every year you'll have more irises," Mémère says.
"They'll spread and fill your yard with beautiful color."
"Yes!" I tell them. "We'll be just like *Miss Rumphius*
in my favorite book—
making the world more beautiful."

WHAT SURVIVAL MEANS

Trowels in hand, knees in the dirt,
Mama, Brooke, and I move small piles of earth,
making space in the ground for the bulbs.
Jenna helps by covering them up.
The iris bulbs don't look like much yet,
but after they sleep under a blanket of snow
through the darkness of winter,
they'll rise up and bloom.
Mémère says the hard winter
will make them
stronger.
People say
what Daddy did to us
made us stronger,
but what if we were already
strong enough?

A NEW PAGE

In September, the leaves change—
turning into blazing oranges, reds, and yellows.
Mama takes a photo for the first day of sixth grade.
She likes to take our pictures for each first day of school
even though we homeschool.
We always make a sign with our grade on it.
Then, after we take the picture, we start school.
This year, we have brand-new books
waiting for us to be the first to fill them in.
Other years, our books were used and torn.
For some subjects we didn't even have books.
Mama taught me to read with little cards she made herself.
Having new books is another nice new thing I like.

CO-OP

Mama decided we should try a homeschooling co-op
so we'll have a chance to be around
other homeschooled kids.
We will have a few classes
each Friday
at the community center.
My grade's classes this semester are
cooking, taught by a mom,
storytelling, also taught by a mom,
and survival skills, taught by a dad.
Mama teaches art for Jenna's grade group,
so Jenna stays with her
while I go to my classes on my own.
In survival skills,
we learn about native plants and animal tracks.
We walk on nearby trails and learn what to do
if we ever get lost in the woods
or need to take care of someone who's hurt.
When a classmate can't keep up, Mr. James
doesn't get mad.
He helps him up, asking, "Are you okay?"
I watch, surprised that this dad really means it.

WHAT IS REALITY?

Thinking about the way Mr. James at co-op is so kind
makes me sad.
While Mémère is having tea with us, I ask her,
"What did you think of Daddy?"
She looks surprised by the question and takes a minute to speak.
"Your dad was a complex person.
Nice on the outside,
nice to us and to strangers,
so we thought we knew him.
But I don't think we ever knew the real him.
He was good at hiding his troubles
from everyone but you, Jenna, and your mama."
Mémère's words make me realize that Daddy
not only made a wall around us
but around himself,
not letting the real him out—
except with us.

SAND TRAY

In my first meeting with my new therapist,
Ms. Danah takes the lid off the table between us,
and it's full of sand.
"You can choose items from the shelf
and arrange them
however you want.
I'd love to see what you create," she says.
I pick out some small trees,
some grass and flowers,
a bridge and stones, and
a dog, a cat, and two girls.
There's even a tiny pencil and books,
so of course I take those.
I arrange the stones in a line down the center.
I leave everything blank on one side
and set up the other side until it feels right.
The girls are sitting with
the dog and cat and pencil and books
under the tree. Pretty flowers are next to them.
"I think I'm done," I say.
"Nice!" Ms. Danah says.
It *is* nice. I like how it feels
to build my own world.

VISITING

Today is the first time that I'm going to spend
the afternoon at Brooke's and stay for dinner.
Mama has never let me before.
Even though Brooke's house is
in the same driveway as ours,
Mama still looks nervous.
Maybe I'm a little nervous too.
I'm glad Mama is just across the street.
Brooke's mom plays music while she makes dinner,
and we all dance around the kitchen.
She even keeps it on through dinner
and while we have mint chocolate chip ice cream
for dessert.
It feels like a party.
I start thinking about Mama and Jenna
and how I know they're not dancing
but sitting alone.
Maybe tomorrow night,
I'll turn on the radio and
play music for Mama.

RETURNING

Even though I had fun at Brooke's,
the feeling I get
when Mama wraps me up
in a warm towel right out of the dryer
is what it feels like to
come back
home.

APPLE PICKING

We are going on our first-ever field trip
with the co-op—
apple picking!
We've never been to an orchard,
and it is amazing,
with rows and rows of trees.
Jenna and I run up the hill,
through the grassy aisles.
My apple basket flips and flops as we run
between
the Golden Delicious and McIntosh trees.
Jenna and I pick the biggest apples
before they fall, heavy, to the ground.
Jenna takes bites out of too many and
puts those in Mama's bag.
Our group stops for a rest, and we sit on a big blanket.
I take out my nature journal
and draw a big juicy apple,
labeling it *Red Delicious*.
A kid next to me takes out their notebook
and draws an apple too.
"Good idea," they say.
"Thanks," I reply.
"You're Lacey, right?" they ask.

"Yeah, what's your name?" I ask.

"Winter," they reply.

"I like that name," I say.

"Can I borrow that red pencil?" Winter asks.

"Sure!" I say, handing it over.

When we're done, we admire each other's art.

When we walked into the orchard,

I stuck close to Mama and Jenna.

But when we leave, Winter and I walk

out of the orchard together.

Just like that, I've made a second friend.

It's getting easier every time.

FALLING *into the* SADDEST KIND *of* SAD

Jenna's kitten, Marble, stops eating
and just wants to sleep,
so Mama calls the vet, and
we bring Marble in.
After the doctors run some tests,
we go home and wait for the results.
Mittens snuggles close to Marble.
They curl up together on the floor with
their heads resting on each other,
and their tails form a heart.
The next day, the vet calls.
Marble has FIP, they say.
Feline infectious peritonitis.
Nothing they can do to help him, they say.
They're sorry, they say.
Just make him comfortable.
We give Marble a soft pink pillow.
He lies on it and barely moves.
Jenna gives him a stuffed animal that he
hugs with his paws,
and she tucks him in with a blue fleece blanket.
She refuses to leave his side, so
we make her a bed
on the floor next to him.
Mittens won't leave Marble's side either.

At midnight, I wake up
and hear Marble coughing.
I find Mama is on the floor too.
Mama holds Jenna and
Jenna holds Marble as he slowly fades.
We all cry when he goes still.
"I'm sorry," Mama offers. "I'm so sorry."
We let go of
all the tears
we've been saving
since *before*.

BECOMING

Mittens sits in the big picture window,
looking out at us as we bury Marble.
Pépère digs a hole and gently lowers the box.
We all put a small handful of dirt over the box,
wiping tears with tissues.
I paint Marble's name on a wide, flat stone.
Jenna paints flowers around his name.
And then we lay the stone on the ground.
When spring comes, we'll plant real flowers
near the stone
so Marble will have a pretty spot to rest in and
he will become part
of the flowers.

BROKEN APART

The next morning, I get up and stare
out the window
like Mittens did the day before.
Marble is buried under a soft gray sky.
Mittens jumps up on the windowsill.
As I pet him, my tears return.
I want to be mad.
Not sad.
Sad feels like anyone can hurt you.
Mad feels like I'm keeping watch.
"It's not fair!" I blurt out,
 deciding I will be mad.
Daddy was always mad.
It worked for him.
I never saw him sad.
He lived his whole life mad.
Tried to burn my toys mad.
Hit Mac mad.
Threw glasses at the wall mad.
Ripped Mama's drawings mad.
Called her names I try to forget mad.
Made Jenna cry mad.
Made me mad mad
forever.

I run to the couch and hit the pillows
since we don't have
the punching bag.
"Lacey," Mama asks, "what's going on?"
She follows me to my room.
Thunder cracks outside the window,
and the sky that was light gray is now
filled with angry, rolling, charcoal-colored clouds.
As the rain releases from the sky,
I fall into Mama's arms
and cry some more.

SORRY

Mama keeps saying she's sorry,
as if it's her fault that Marble got sick.
May and Norah said they were sorry too.
Everyone is always sorry for everything,
but bad things still happen.

SECOND CHANCES

We drive back to the shelter
so Jenna can choose another kitten.
A lady with a long braid greets us at the door.
"Please come in," she says. "I'm so sorry for your loss."
We walk through the door with the cat silhouette
and wander slowly down the hall
until Jenna stops
and points at a teeny dark-gray kitten
with a white stripe on her nose and white paws.
Like Mittens.
The lady clicks the door open, and when we enter,
the kitten looks up at Jenna with large eyes
and crouches down smaller.
"This one seems really scared all the time," the lady says
as Jenna picks up the kitten
and holds her close.
"But she seems to like you."
Jenna nods, and the lady smiles.
"Okay, then, sweetie. She's yours."
Mama fills out the adoption papers, and
as we put the new kitten in her carrier, I think that
Second Chances is a good name
for this place.

REUNITED

We start walking toward the door to leave,
but before we get there, I stop.
A familiar bark floats to my ears.
And another one.
That sounds a lot like—
Mac!
I set down the carrier, turn around, and run back
toward the door with a dog silhouette.
"Lacey, where are you going?" Mama says, following me.
"It's Mac," I shout, not stopping for a second.
"He's here."
"No, it couldn't be, Lacey," says Mama,
but there's a hint of question in her voice.
Bark!
"It's him!" I reach the door, swing it open,
and enter a hallway filled with cages of dogs on both sides.
Rows of dogs watch me run by.
Bark!
"Lacey!" Mama runs after me with Jenna on her hip.
Then I stop running
because
I see
Mac.
He's got his face as close to the cage as he can get it
while barking at me to come let him out.

He's thin and frantic,

and the best sight ever.

I kneel down to him, and a worker comes over.

"Can I help you?"

"Yes, this is our dog!" I say. "We need to bring him home."

"I can't believe it," Mama says. "Mac, we missed you so much!"

The worker unlocks Mac's gate and

attaches a leash to his collar.

Mac tries to jump toward me,

and the worker says,

"He's excited now, but

it may take some time for him

to actually warm up to you.

I think he might have been hurt before."

I know exactly how Mac has been hurt.

"Yes," I tell her. "He was hurt, but

he'll be safe now with us."

Mac licks my hand. My buddy. Our Mac.

Jenna, who's smiling,

reaches out and strokes Mac.

"Mac," she says quietly.

Her first word.

Mac.

UNFAMILIAR

Until now,
I've never seen Mittens prick up the hairs on his back.
He is the only one *not* happy to see Mac.
We decide that Mittens will sleep in my room tonight,
Jenna's new kitten will sleep with her, in her room,
and Mac can have the rest of the house.
They'll have to sort this out
eventually.

BECOMING FRIENDS

Jenna looks at the photo album we made her,
full of pictures of Marble.
Her new kitten snuggles into her, and
Mac comes over and crouches down
next to them.
It's as if they both know
how much Jenna needs them.
"Mac," Jenna says.
Then she lifts one of her kitten's white paws
and waves it at Mac.
"Snowpaws," she says slowly, as if she's
introducing them, assuming they'll be friends.
And she's right.
It's not long before
the three of them are snuggling.
With my kitten, it's not so easy.
Mac sniffs Mittens.
Mittens, his fur on end again,
stares down Mac.
Snarling,
hissing,
twirling.
Finally, Mac walks away.
Later, they circle each other
until Mac tucks his tail in and lies down.

Then Mittens does the same.

They've reached an understanding.

Watching those two figure out their new world

makes me remember Mémère's words—

some things just need to take their own sweet time.

HIGHER

Jenna loves our swing set so much
that she wants me to push her
for what feels like hours.
Mac runs and plays around us,
enjoying his new yard.
Then he sits by us, almost like
he's keeping watch.
The sun warms my face,
but the air is crisp and feels good.
It's fleece jacket and gloves weather.
Jenna giggles.
"Higher!" she demands.
Hearing her speak
is worth pushing her
for however long she likes.
"Higher," she says again,
so higher it is!

EVERYONE THINKS *That* WE'RE OKAY NOW

They say we've come so far.
They say we've changed so much.
And we have.
But at the same time, so much is the same inside.
My heart pounds when I hear
a loud sound that reminds me of
Daddy slamming the walls.
Or a diesel truck—*the sound of him coming home*—
or when Mama moves the curtain just enough
to peek out the window—*like she's scared*—and then
I'm scared too.
Sometimes I wish we could be like other kids
and do ordinary things with a mama who's not
always afraid of everything.
Sometimes I'm afraid of everything too.
Outside my window I see the first snowflake fall,
and it brings a surge of hope.
This winter *will* be different
because it's the first we're not shut in.
I step outside,
cup my hands and catch snowflakes,
studying them
until they melt
into drops of ice water on my skin.

PANIC

Pépère and Mémère bring all of us
to the botanical gardens light show.
We wander along glowing pathways
under glistening arbors.
Each step is a new discovery, like a dream world
where the lights flicker like fireflies.
But then the lights feel too bright.
I can't keep track of all the people walking by.
Too many faces to scan.
What if *he's* here?
My heartbeat echoes in my head.
The world starts to spin.
I reach for Mama's hand.
She looks at me and knows it's time to leave.
As we head for the exit, she says something
hushed to Mémère and Pépère.
If they're disappointed, they don't say so.
But the guilt washes over me anyway,
and I can't stop the panic.
Even though we keep trying
new things that we couldn't do *before*,
sometimes it's the new things
that remind me of *before*
because of why they're new.

I'D RATHER BE HOME

When *before* memories creep up on me,
I have to be alone,
where it is quiet and the walls are
familiar and safe,
so I can fight the memories
that try to push their way
into now—
so I can tell them to
go back
to
before.

COURT

Mama says she has to go to court to testify
on the witness stand
in front of a group of people
called a jury, who will
decide on a verdict
about whether or not Daddy stays in jail.
She is going without us.
Daddy will be there.
For the first time in a long time,
my heart pounds when she leaves.
I thought getting better meant
always
getting better,
but it doesn't.

ALL OVER

Mama comes home just before dinner.
We have the table all set, and
the dinner we helped
Mémère make is
on the stove, but
Mama doesn't see.
The look on Mama's face is
so pale, so tired, so drained.
I run to her.
Jenna too, in tears.
Mama starts crying.
Mémère hugs her.
I want to ask her about the trial
but can't find the words,
so I sit there quietly
while she and Jenna cry.

FORGETTING IT ALL

The snow blankets the hills in softness.
Jenna and I pull on our snowsuits, mittens, and hats,
grab our blue plastic sled, and
start at the top of Mémère and Pépère's hill,
taking in our snowy kingdom.
Mac runs in the sparkly fluff, rolling around and eating it.
He LEAPS! and lands like a winter rabbit.
As the sun starts to sink behind the trees,
the sky transforms into the color of Creamsicles,
changing the snow color too.
Sitting in the sled
with Jenna in front of me,
I push us off with my bright pink mittens
and we glide down the snowy hill
away from thinking of everything else
that I don't want to remember.
Mac follows, with fluffs of snow
decorating his nose like frosting.
How did we ever find each other again?
My hearts fills with warmth.
Glad I heard his bark that day.
Glad he heard us and called out.
Mama follows us, running
down the hill, laughing.

The SUN RISES

Maine winters last longer than summers,

but today, out my window, the sun is melting the snow.

Green buds are poking through

where winter has already disappeared.

In the afternoon, Brooke comes over

and we dance around

the backyard, excited by the promise of spring.

We watch the robins dance too,

then they stop,

listen,

peck at the ground,

and dance again.

The air feels soft, and a light rain

begins to fall.

We turn our faces to the sky

as the sun returns.

This kind of light is my favorite kind,

when the shadows are long and

the trees are golden against the deep blue sky.

Each season, each day holds its own beauty that

feels like another kind of warm hug.

NEW

Mama says she has one last court hearing,
but this time, it's not about Daddy.
It's about us. All of us.
She's going to get us a new last name!
Mama's maiden name: Dawn.
At first, I had wanted to keep the name
I was born with; it was mine.
But now I want to have a last name that shows how far
we've come. How we are beginning.
Dawn.

GROWING

The air smells of fresh-cut grass as Brooke and
I survey our garden.
Our iris shoots have started pointing up
from the bulbs we planted last fall.
Hostas transplanted from Mémère's garden
peek out through the dirt too.
Soon Mémère's friend Sharron is going to give us
marigolds, grape hyacinths, and lobelias to plant.
I love saying all the different names.
Then I remember what else we have to add!
I run and find my sunflower seeds from Virginia
and the spade that was a gift from Mémère.
We select the perfect spot.
I dig small beds for the seeds,
then Brooke tucks them in with soft earth.
We give them each a drink of water.
I draw a sunflower on a Popsicle stick I saved,
and we mark the seeds in the ground.
Our dreamed-about garden is becoming real.

MY OWN NAME

Today I'm getting my very own library card!
Walking into the building, I feel
like I'm entering
my very own kingdom.
Books stack up tall on the walls
in rows like a rainbow,
offering stories that will take me to other lands,
other worlds.
The librarian hands me a slip of paper to fill out,
and on the line that says *Name*,
I carefully print *Lacey Dawn*.
It feels like a new start,
a new day.
Then the librarian shows me
how to look up books
and how to make requests with
my own library card
in my own name:
Lacey Dawn.
My new name, my real name, me.

FIDDLEHEADS

Whenever Mama has a meeting or
needs a quiet space to work,
we go to Pépère and Mémère's.
Jenna is used to this and is fine with it now.
Today when we arrive, Pépère asks, "Have you ever
tried a fiddlehead?"
We look at each other and shake our heads.
"What's a fiddlehead?" I ask.
"Put your muck boots on and we'll show you," he says.
Mémère gives us each a small basket.
She holds Jenna's hand, and
we all hike out through the field
and into the woods, until
we reach the river.
Pépère explains that
we are looking for clumps of special ferns
that haven't unfurled yet.
"At this stage," he tells us, "when they are still furled fronds,
you can eat them.
You girls are going to have a treat for supper!"
Jenna and I are really good at
picking fiddleheads.
Soon our baskets are full.
When we get back,

Mémère fills the sink with cold water
and shows us how to
wash them and remove the shiny,
papery brown husks.
Then we steam the fiddleheads, "Just long enough,"
Mémère says, "to be tender, but snappy."
We sit down for dinner,
and when I try one,
I love how green and fresh they taste.
Jenna puts more melted butter on hers
and eats them all up too.
"Furled fronds," Jenna says, and we all nod at her,
smiling.
"Fiddleheads," I say, "are my new favorite."
A spiral of spring on my plate.

SUNFLOWER

I run outside most days with Mac to check on
my sunflower seeds.
Nothing yet. I'm confused.
There should be small green shoots by now.
My hearts sinks, and I figure that the seeds
weren't quite ready yet when I pulled them out.
That's why they were so pale and soft, not striped.
Then Pépère comes over with a surprise for me.
When Mac runs to greet him, Pépère holds
the small potted plant
out of Mac's way with one hand and pets him with the other.
"I know someone loves sunflowers, so I planted this for you
from seeds I saved last summer," he tells me.
"After Mémère told me you had to leave your flower in Virginia,
I figured you might want one here at your new home."
It's the nicest gift, and I thank Pépère for being so thoughtful.
"I kept it until it was ready for you to plant," he adds, "so you can
do that in the next day or two."
Jenna reaches up for the sprout, so I lower it for her to see.
"Lacey's sun," she says.
I almost fall over—it's the first time she has said my name!
Now this sunflower is even more special to me.

SHUTTING OUTSIDE OUT

Waking up and seeing my sunflower sprout on
my windowsill makes me happy.
I pull out a soft-green colored pencil
and sketch it, its new leaves reaching to the light.
Mittens tries to nibble the end of my pencil.
But even with that,
when I'm finished, I think this is
my best sketch yet.
My art is getting better each time I draw.
Walking into the kitchen to
show Mama my drawing,
I see her putting down her phone.
Her face has gone pale.
"Mama?" I ask.
She doesn't answer.
Suddenly, without a word,
she scrambles to the shut the curtains.
Shuts more curtains.
Walks to my room.
Shuts those.
"What is it?" I try to ask again.
When she turns around, we stare face-to-face.
"He's out," she whispers in a panic.
"Out of jail."

My feet freeze where they are,

and I can't move.

The sudden thought of *him*,

coming here . . .

"I don't know if he knows where we live," she says,

as if she knows what I'm thinking.

"But just in case,

we're staying inside today."

I walk back into my room,

plop down on my bed,

and hug Diamond, my deer.

Not this again.

Staying inside.

Afraid of *him* again.

Crowded together in a dark house.

Prisoners again.

This life was supposed to be different.

It was good.

I tighten my fists.

Tears sting, but I hold them back.

I wanted to go outside and

plant my sunflower

but know that I can't.

The WORLD CLOSES IN

Police keep calling and driving by.
Mama keeps talking with them
but doesn't say much to anyone else.
Pépère and Mémère say they're on the lookout.
They won't let anything happen to us.
Our neighbors say that too.
Mama tries to keep the curtains closed,
but Mac likes to nose the hem, and they open a little.
He wants to be outside.
Then Mama adjusts them again to close off
any view of the outside world.
They both do this over and over again.
The day goes by and then another.
All I can do is water my sunflower and move it around
into windows that have sunlight
on the other side of the curtains.
Mac is pacing.
He needs to run.
My sunflower sprout's wilting.
It needs more sun.

STEPPING OUT

The third morning, the sun calls me outside.
Suddenly, I don't care if
Daddy is out there
waiting for us or not.
My garden is withering,
wanting water.
My sunflower is waiting
for earth to spread its roots.
Inside the house, I'm tired of waiting
for Mama to be okay
again.
She might keep on worrying,
but I can't keep on living in the
dark.
I can't go back to *before*
when I know we can have *after*.

I take a deep breath,
then walk around the house,
opening the curtains,
letting the sunlight fall
onto all of us.
When I open the living room window,
I'm surprised to see

Mémère and Pépère and
Brooke and her mom
in our yard,
talking with one another.
They see me looking out and
wave for me to come outside.
I give them a thumbs-up, then
go sit next to Mama on the couch.
She's so sad and afraid.
But I tell her,
"Mama, everyone is here for us."
We get up
and walk to the window together.
I show her, and they wave again.
"Let's go outside," I say.
I gather my stuff, and Mama gathers Jenna.
With my sunflower and spade in hand,
I step out the door with them.
Mac follows us, skipping into the yard.
Brooke runs over to meet me, and
Mémère and Pépère huddle around Mama.
We all walk to the garden together.
He might be out there
somewhere,
but that doesn't mean
we can't be out here too.

SUNLIGHT

I kneel down in our garden
and move the rich earth,
digging a hole with my spade,
then carefully let the fragile,
pot-bound sunflower
fall out into my hands and
into the ground.
I softly pat dirt around it,
then sprinkle it with water,
giving it the best chance
at life that I can.
I stand up
and walk over to join everyone.
Surrounded by their love
in this world we've built together,
I feel safe
and free
to grow
and bloom.

AUTHOR'S NOTE

Dear Reader,

I wrote this book to send a message of hope. Sometimes we have to go through some tough stuff to make it to the other side. That's what happened to me—and to the family in my book. Thank you for taking this journey with us and for making it to the other side.

While some of the events in this book might seem unbelievable, they are based in fact. And while this book is not an autobiography, the story was inspired by my own experiences as a survivor of over a decade of domestic abuse. This book covers many different kinds of abuse, such as psychological and emotional. Abuse is not always a visible bruise or a physical injury. Sometimes you can't see the injuries, but they are there just the same.

You might have questions about what defines abuse, how to help a friend, or how to start a conversation about something you're going through. As soon as you can, talk to someone you trust: a parent, a teacher, or a doctor. You can also call one of the numbers below. The first step is breaking the silence.

I mention Caring Unlimited in this book, with permission, because it is the organization that helped me in my local area, but the hotlines below are also here for you wherever you are in the United States, twenty-four hours a day, seven days a week.

National Domestic Violence Hotline

thehotline.org

Call 1-800-799-SAFE (7233) or text "START" to 88788

National Child Abuse Hotline

childhelphotline.org

Call or text 1-800-422-4453

Caring Unlimited (York County, Maine)

caring-unlimited.org

Call 1-800-239-7298

ACKNOWLEDGMENTS

Creating a book doesn't happen alone. It takes time, support, and a community. Many amazing people have helped me along the way. I couldn't have completed this book without them.

Thank you to Ron Gobeil, my high school art teacher, for encouraging me to develop my craft, providing opportunities like the Heartwood School of Art, and cheering on my career from the start. Thank you to all my professors and friends at the Rhode Island School of Design for introducing me to the world of illustration and children's literature and for being tough and kind at the same time.

My heartfelt thank-you to Hillary Homzie for her gentle care of a fragile idea. This novel began in her Hollins class as a tiny seed of a poem, then bloomed into something more. Thank you so much to Cece Bell for her insightful feedback on early pages and for introducing me to the world of novels in verse by suggesting that I read Jacqueline Woodson's *Brown Girl Dreaming*. A special thank-you to Candice Ransom for not only editing the first draft of this book in 2017 (what a job!) but for compelling me to find a backbone and stop the tears. I'm so thankful for women like her, who have the grit to encourage others to find theirs. Thank you to the entirety of Hollins University, specifically my many tremendous mentors—Ruth Sanderson, Amanda Cockrell, Tony Neuron, Lisa Fraustino, Elizabeth Dulemba, Ashley Wolff, Lauren Mills, Dennis Nolan, Julie Pfeiffer, Alexandria LaFaye, and more.

Thank you so much to MJ Begin for encouraging me to "own it" and for her years of friendship. Working with MJ at both RISD and Hollins has influenced me professionally and personally. My journey to Hollins, and this book, wouldn't have happened if not for Ashley Wolff—all because I read her picture book *Each Living Thing* to my daughters and reached out. I'm so glad she suggested I apply to Hollins and chase my dreams! Thank you to my Hollins friends and classmates Lucy Rowe, Kassy Keppol, Karylynn Keppol, Cassie Gustafson, Lorian Tu, Jessie Cole Jackson, Jennifer Luevanos, and the crew for their friendship and feedback along the way. Thank you to the Keppol kids for hanging out with my daughters, making flower crowns, wading in the creek, and playing hide-and-seek during our early days at Hollins. Thank you to Pop's Ice Cream for the many strange grilled cheese sandwiches and ice cream floats on paper lace doilies!

Thank you to the Society of Children's Books Writers and Illustrators for providing opportunities and for championing the world of children's literature. Thank you so much to Brian Lies for his friendship, encouragement, guidance, and support. Working together during the New England SCBWI 4x4 Mentorship Program helped shape my work into what it is today, down to the graphite dust drawings in this book. Thank you to Heidi Stemple for her encouragement and author sisterhood, Melissa Sweet for phone conversations that left me inspired, and Lynda Mullaly Hunt for making me feel at home at Nancy Paulsen Books and for being an amazing human.

Thank you to the entire Susan P. Bloom committee for awarding this book the 2019 Susan P. Bloom Discovery Award.

Thank you to the McArthur Public Library team—Deanna, Deb, Kathy, John, Melanie, Renee, Jackie, Jane, Jeff, and everyone—for being so supportive and amazing. Thank you to Kim Campbell and the folks at South Portland Public Library, as well as Print: A Bookstore and Kirsten Cappy of Curious City. Thank you to my picture book critique pals, Carey Johnson, Jessie Goodwin, Michelle Smith, and Dorson Plourde, for always being there to provide notes and jokes. A special thank-you to my verse critique group, Kip Wilson, Rebecca Caprara, and Krista Surprenant, for your wise and thoughtful notes and support. Thank you to the local authors and illustrators of New England for creating a community that welcomes others in: Jess Keating, John Schu, Josh Funk, Lily Williams, Julie Falatko, Liz Goulet Dubois, Lynnor Bontigao, Rajani LaRocca, Teresa Robeson, Sylvia Liu, Leo Quiles, Sarah Lynne Ruel, Russ Cox, Ann Braden, Jarett Lerner, Abi Cushman, Amanda Davis, Anne Appert, Janae Marks, and so many more! Thank you to Bonnie Christine and her community for their creative support, encouragement, and always-savvy business advice. Thank you to Nick Lund of Maine Audubon for his article *A Word on the Capitalization of Bird Names.*

Thank you to the entire local community of family, friends, and strangers who came together to help us leave and rebuild our lives. Thank you to the Biddeford Police Department, the

Maine State Police, Child Protective Services workers, the guardian ad litem, attorneys, therapists, and more for coming together and helping my daughters and me escape and move forward. On the day we left, our life began again. A special thank-you to Sarah D. for being a warrior for our case from the beginning. Thank you to Caring Unlimited for providing a place for us to recover and rebuild our lives. My sincere thanks to the Women's Independence Scholarship Program for supporting the dreams of survivors like myself. Thank you to Patrisha McLean of *Finding Our Voices* and the crew at Storm Warriors for helping survivors share their stories.

Thank you to Kat Rushall for encouraging me to keep going in my early days! Thank you to Wendi Gu for believing in my work and seeing this project into Nancy's hands. Thank you to the one and only Paige Terlip, my stellar agent at the Andrea Brown Literary Agency, for being my open door in the agency I've long had starry eyes for, and for wanting to collaborate with me. I can't wait to see all the books we will bring into this book world together. We make a great team! Thank you to Victoria Piontek, Kelly Sonnack, and everyone at ABLA.

Thank you to my outstanding editor, Nancy Paulsen, for saying YES to this book; for her brilliance, insight, spot-on feedback, patience, and ruthless word-cutting skills; for knowing just the right words to keep or let go of, allowing the sky to get darker so the stars could shine brighter; for bringing this book to life; and for being willing to take on the tough stuff. I couldn't have done this without you! Thank you to Sara LaFleur; Marikka Tamura for her art direction and inspiration; Cindy Howle for her sharp copyediting eye and thoughtful insight; and the entire team at Nancy Paulsen Books/Penguin Random House.

Thank you to Mom and Dad for so many things. Too many to list. Mom for homeschooling me, for allowing me to become the wild nature child that I needed to be, and for always being there. And Dad for always encouraging me, building art displays, and teaching me about the woods, twisted trees, hard work, and the love of nature. Thank you to my sister Erica for making the trip with us to Hollins and being with my girls, and to my other siblings, Chris, Ashley, Colleen, and Angela, for their support and encouragement. Thank you to my grandparents James and Therese Lowell for passing on a love of the wild Maine woods and for sharing life with us, and to my late grandmother, Lucy Buck, for being such an inspiring spitfire and telling me to "get that divorce." Thank you also to my dear friends Brooke Larrabee, for her years of friendship and for letting me be weird; Mary Guignard, for always being a beacon of strength and for basil; and Sharron Paquereau, for being there and for irises. Thank you to Jake and Kellie for their friendship and encouragement. A special thank-you to Jack Doyle for his support.

Thank you to my husband, Scott, for his never-ending support and encouragement, for understanding my endless work hours and love of this craft, and for providing many cups of coffee and a continuous supply of chocolate.

Thank you immensely to my daughters for being the reason

why I left our world of *before* and the reason I keep fighting and rebuilding our *after*. Keep being you and shine your lights, both of you. You inspire me each day, and I love you.

Thank you to anyone who has helped someone recover, rebuild, start over, or stand up again. And to those who have had to start over from anything, rebuild, or stand up again—you are all heroes.

Thank you to everyone listed here, and more, for helping us find our road to after.